Where's Jenna?

For Jenna

ACKNOWLEDGMENTS

*This book would not have been possible
without the enthusiastic cooperation, endless
patience, and good humor of Jenna, Kyle,
Cindy and Neil Rappaport.*

—MM

SIMON & SCHUSTER BOOKS FOR YOUNG READERS
1230 Avenue of the Americas, New York, New York 10020
Copyright © 1994 by Margaret Miller. All rights reserved
including the right of reproduction in whole or
in part in any form.
SIMON & SCHUSTER BOOKS FOR YOUNG READERS
is a trademark of Simon & Schuster.
Designed by Paul Zakris.
The text for this book is set in New Baskerville.
Manufactured in the United States of America
10 9 8 7 6 5 4 3 2 1

Library of Congress Cataloging–in–Publication Data
Miller, Margaret.
 Where's Jenna? / by Margaret Miller
    p.   cm.
 Summary: The story about a young girl's parents
who are trying to get her to take her bath presents such
prepositions as "around," "behind," and "outside,"
showing them in bold type.
 [1. Baths—Fiction. 2. English language—Prepositions—
Fiction.]   I. Title.
PZ7.M628Wi   1994   [E]—dc20   93-13981   CIP
ISBN: 0-671-79167-2

Where's Jenna?

By Margaret Miller

SIMON & SCHUSTER BOOKS FOR YOUNG READERS
Published by Simon & Schuster
New York ✦ London ✦ Toronto ✦ Sydney ✦ Tokyo ✦ Singapore

"Jenna, where are you?
It's time for your bath."

Jenna's mother heard a giggle
and looked **behind** the door.

No Jenna—just a blue hat
on the doorknob.

Her mother heard Jenna's
baby brother laugh and peeked
under the blanket.

No Jenna—just two red shoes
between the stuffed animals.

Jenna's mother heard a splash
and turned **toward** the goldfish.

No Jenna—just two yellow socks
on top of the aquarium.

Her mother heard a squeaky hinge and reached **inside** the toy chest.

No Jenna—just a pair of green pants **among** the toys.

Jenna's mother heard footsteps
and walked **down** the stairs.

No Jenna—just a pink shirt
on the step **below**.

Jenna's father hummed
a lullaby while she kneeled
beside the couch.

Jenna put her arms
around her father.
"Guess who," she said.

"Are you the little girl who should
be walking **up** the stairs to take a bath?"

"No," said Jenna, crawling **beneath**
her father's legs. "I'm a tiger who
has come to visit her baby brother."

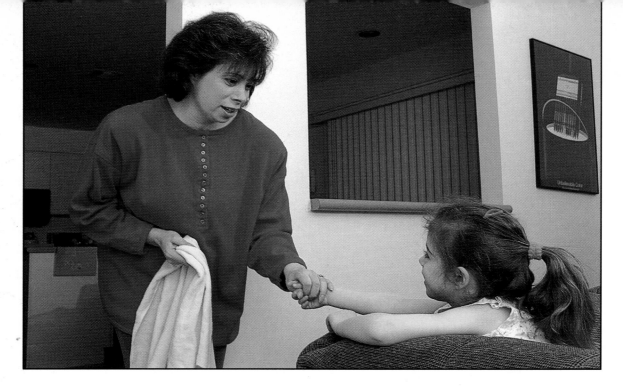

"Even tigers need to take baths," said her mother as she walked **into** the room.

"Rub-a-dub-dub, sweet Jenna **in** the tub," said her mother and father.

Jenna put her teddy bear **next to** her baby brother. "Teddy will keep him company while I'm taking my bath," she said.

Jenna stood **outside** the bathroom door. "Hurry up, Mom! What's taking you so long?"